Whose List Is This?

By Andrea Butler
Illustrated by John Sandford

CelebrationPress

An Imprint of ScottForesman
A Division of HarperCollinsPublishers

2

3

4

7

It's mine.

8

DAGMAR SCHULTZ AND THE GREEN-EYED MONSTER

DAGMAR SCHULTZ AND THE GREEN-EYED MONSTER

LYNN HALL

Charles Scribner's Sons · New York
Collier Macmillan Canada · Toronto
Maxwell Macmillan International
New York · Oxford · Singapore · Sydney

Charles Scribner's Sons Books for Young Readers
Macmillan Publishing Company
866 Third Avenue, New York, NY 10022

Collier Macmillan Canada, Inc.
1200 Eglinton Avenue East, Suite 200
Don Mills, Ontario M3C 3N1

First edition   1 2 3 4 5 6 7 8 9 10
Printed in the United States of America

Library of Congress Cataloging-in-Publication Data
Hall, Lynn.
Dagmar Schultz and the green-eyed monster / Lynn Hall.
— 1st ed.   p.   cm.
    Summary: Jealous of a pretty and popular new student,
thirteen-year-old Dagmar decides to get even with humorous results.
ISBN 0-684-19254-3
[1. Jealousy—Fiction.   2. Iowa—Fiction.
3. Humorous stories.]   I. Title.
PZ7.H1458Daf   1991   [Fic]—dc20   90–43524

DAGMAR SCHULTZ AND THE GREEN-EYED MONSTER

One

Two things happened to me in December, one good and one rotten. One thing meant years of bother and yuckiness. That was the good thing.

The rotten thing was beautiful and charming and loved by one and all . . . except me. Her name was Ashley Fingerhut, and she had better hair than I did, so I started off hating her.

Actually, three things happened to me in December, but the third was so weird, I'll have to lead up to that part of the story gradually or you're going to write me off as a totally crazy person.

It started with Ashley. Even her name made me sick. Dagmar is such a terrific, glamorous name, I never thought anybody in New Berlin,

1

Iowa, would ever be able to top it, much less anybody in my own eighth grade. The Schultz part of my name isn't so hot, but I expect to marry a rich guy with a name like Merriwether or Du Pont. Dagmar Du Pont. . . . That's New *Ber*lin, pronounced like Merlin. Don't ask me why.

But Ashley—now there's a name to have to compete with. Especially with all the other stuff that went along with it. For one thing, she was new in town, and since New Berlin has only three hundred people, any new family causes lots of excitement.

Ashley's father was the new postmaster. He got transferred up here from Cedar Rapids, so Ashley also had the advantage of being from a city. And nobody knew if her mother was dead or just divorced, so there was the element of mystery.

And she was cute. I had to give her that. She had sort of a round face with round eyes and nose and mouth and a disgustingly cute, round little figure. Waistline and everything. I was thirteen years, one month old at the time, and I was just beginning to be able to feel a little dent starting around my middle, but it didn't show yet unless I strangled myself with my belt. Then Mom would yell at me for cutting off my circulation, and Gramma Schultz would start telling horrible stories of women who had deformed babies because they wore corsets while they were pregnant.

But the worst thing about Ashley Fingerhut was her hair. It was longer than mine, it was blonder than mine, and—get this!—it was naturally curly. Naturally curly. I couldn't stand it.

My hair has always been my best body part. So far. It's long enough to sit on if I do a backbend and crack my neck a little bit. It's almost blond and it'll be a lot blonder as soon as I'm old enough to do what I want with it. But it is dead straight. I never minded its being dead straight before. But now, all of a sudden, it looked ugly. And it was the best part of me.

I didn't know if I was going to be strong enough for all the crushers life had in store for me.

The other worst thing about Ashley was that she was so nice. I couldn't even hate her for being stuck-up. She was kind of quiet and smiley and unsure of herself, like you're supposed to be if you're the new kid in town.

So of course my mom and my aunt Dorothy invited Ashley and her father home for Sunday dinner after church that first day after they moved to town.

Mom said, "You're just the same age as our Dagmar. She'll love having a new friend in town."

And Aunt Dorothy said, "No bother at all. We always have the whole family for Sunday dinner. Another two mouths to feed won't even be noticed."

We were all standing on the steps of the Methodist church, sorting ourselves out into families and waiting for my little sister George-Ann to come out. She sang in the Angel Choir, and it always took her forever to get out of her robe. She loved dressing up in that robe.

It was a dazzling, bright morning with new snow and sunshine all over the place. I should have felt great, but I'd just spent an hour staring at the back of Ashley's curly head and realizing that I was no longer the most gorgeous young girl in New Berlin.

My cousin Neese poked me in the arm with her dad's car keys and motioned to me. She wasn't necessarily one of my favorite people, but right then I loved her a lot. She was familiar, she was a known part of my old life *before* Ashley . . . and she was fat. Well, large anyway, especially her thighs and her big frizzy hairdo. Her hair was uglier than mine. Yes, definitely, there was one head of hair in New Berlin uglier than mine.

I started after her, glad to get away from the jolly group on the church steps, but then Aunt Dorothy yelled after us, "Take Ashley with you. Show her the countryside."

So instead of a nice ride to Strawberry Point alone with my cousin Neese, griping about Ashley every mile of the way, we had to take her with us.

But we made her sit in the backseat.

Ever since Neese got her driver's license a couple of weeks ago, she and I had been making the Sunday noon Gramma run to Strawberry Point. If you haven't started doing it yet, take my word for it, there is nothing like being in a car without an adult in it. It's a whole different feeling. Like escaping or flying or something. I couldn't help loving the feeling of it, even with Ashley in the backseat.

She leaned forward and said in that sweet voice, "Now let's see, you're Dagmar and you're Denise, right, or is it the other way around?"

For a second there, I started to feel sorry for her. I started imagining what it would be like to be thrown into a whole new world where you didn't know a single person except your dad. I'd lived my whole life in New Berlin, where it was news on the street corners when I finally got toilet trained.

But just as I was getting this sympathy twinge toward her, a little voice in my head said, "She's cuter than you are, Dagmar." And I was right back to hating her again.

Neese and Ashley did most of the talking on the way to town. I sat in the front seat and looked out at the rounded, snowy hills. Everything looked the same as always: white cornfields with tawny stubble of cornstalks sticking up through the snow and black patches of earth on the south slopes; snowmobile tracks in all the roadside ditches; and in the distance, in a hayfield bordered by woods, a herd of a dozen deer browsing along in broad daylight. A snowy Sunday in northeast Iowa. All was peace and beauty.

Except inside me where I was boiling.

Neese drove like the driver ed teacher was right in there with us. Never went over fifty-five, pulled over in the right-hand lane on the uphills, so faster cars could pass us, signaled for turns a whole block ahead of time. I don't know if she thought I was going to tattle on her if she went fifty-seven or if she was just that kind of person. She was probably just that kind of person. She'd go through her whole life at fifty-five miles an hour. I figured I'd spend most of mine being pulled out of ditches.

But we finally made it to Strawberry Point and pulled in at the Lutheran Retirement Home. They had Gramma all wrapped up and waiting just inside the door, but both Neese and I had to go get her and walk her to the car. She was scared to death of falling and breaking her hip again, which was what happened to her two years ago.

"Who's that?" Gramma said as we settled her in the front seat. I got in back with Ashley and slammed the door a little harder than necessary.

Neese did the honors, since she was more polite than I was. "Gramma, this is Ashley Fingerhut. She just moved to town this week. Her father's the new postmaster."

Gramma craned around to look Ashley up and down. Ashley smiled adorably. I slid down in my corner and hid behind my curtain of hair. Straight not-blond hair. Boring-looking, straight, not-blond hair.

"Well, ain't you pretty," Gramma said, hitting the nail right on the thumb. "I bet you'll have all the boys standing on their ears around here. She's going to give you some competition in a few years, Dagmar, when you start getting interested in the boys. You'll have to go some to beat this pretty thing."

Thanks a lot, Gramma, I thought. Just gouge the old knife in a little deeper, give it a couple more twists, see if I'll bleed another bucketful. What are grammas for, anyhow? Love and loyalty and all that stuff. Right.

I looked at Ashley from behind the curtain of my hair. She was wearing a puffy quilted coat of that sort of soft pinky-purply color. Mauve, I think it is. I never say it out loud because I don't know whether it's "mawve" or "mowve," but probably Ashley knew how to say it.

Anyhow, mawve or mowve, the coat made her look all sort of satiny skinned and goldy haired and doll-like. She wasn't wearing lipstick, but her chubby little lips were pink anyhow. And smiling. That was the worst. She was smiling and laughing at something Gramma said. Neese was laughing, too.

I was the only grouch in the bunch. I hated myself for being that way, but I couldn't seem to turn the mood around.

Again there was that little voice in my head. "Get her," the voice said. "She's your enemy. Get her."

Two

That night I was sitting in bed trying to read a Candlelight Romance when my dad came in and sat on my bed. We had the room to ourselves because GeorgeAnn was still in the bathroom. My younger brothers, Cootie, David, and Deaney, were still making noise in their room across the hall. Mom was downstairs in her and Daddy's room with the baby, Delight.

We had so much privacy I was afraid we were in for a serious talk. But it wasn't that bad. Daddy just kind of squeezed my foot and looked at me sympathetically and said, "You didn't seem thrilled with your new friend, honey. You should give her a chance."

I nodded. What I wanted to say was, "Give her a chance to do what, ruin my life?"

"She seems like a very nice little girl. You'll probably get to be best friends one of these days."

"I've got a best friend."

"I know. But wouldn't two be better than one?"

I looked out at him from behind my hair. Usually, Daddy is on my side, but this sounded like he thought I was wrong, just because I hadn't drooled all over Ashley, like the rest of the family.

"Daddy?"

"What?"

"If I decided I wanted to get a permanent, could I?"

"If you really wanted to, but wouldn't that be copying somebody else instead of being your own unique and wonderful self?"

I thought about that for a second, then grinned out at him and felt a little bit better.

That lasted till the next morning on the school bus, when Shelly, my best friend, took the seat beside Ashley so I had to sit behind them. All our lives, Shelly and I have sat together on the bus.

She used to be Mickey when we were kids.

She had real short red curly hair and looked like a boy. Then this past year she quit looking like one and started looking *at* one instead. She went from the Mickey part of her name, Michelle, to the Shelly part, and snapped up the only eligible boy in New Berlin. She didn't really like him— she just didn't want me to get him first.

So now here she was crowding in with Ashley and making me sit in the other seat behind them. Alone.

And when we got to school, it was even worse. Shelly took Ashley to the principal's office to get her signed in. I was going to do that, since I knew Ashley from yesterday and had more of a right to show her around than Shelly did. But there they were, the two curly kids, waltzing into homeroom eight minutes after the bell, with a smirk on Shelly's face and a note from the principal to excuse the tardiness.

The principal himself came along a few minutes later to do the formal introductions. He asked us all to welcome our new class member and make her feel at home. Mr. Ebersole looks like a frog. He does. I'd think that even if he wasn't a school principal. He's short and fat and totally bald, and wears half glasses, just the bottom halves of the lenses. He drops his face into his chins and looks at you over the tops of the glasses, and it is very hard not to break up laughing—mostly because he takes himself so seriously. Anybody that funny looking needs a sense of humor to go along with it.

He finished his speech and left, and our homeroom teacher went back to what he was saying. His name is Mr. Hartung. He is mainly a coach, with a couple of algebra classes on the side because it's too small a school to have a full-time track coach. He doesn't really care about teaching any more than most of us care about learning, especially algebra, so we get along with him very well. We all sort of go our own ways.

His homeroom period is like that, too. The first fifteen minutes of the day is homeroom, and usually we just sort of goof off. But today we did have serious business.

"As I was saying"—Mr. Hartung chopped at the desk with his ruler—"our Christmas dance is this Saturday, which doesn't give us much time for the decoration and refreshment committees to get their acts together. Now that Ashley has joined us, that's one more pair of hands. Right, Ashley?"

She smiled her curly smile and nodded at him. I could see Mr. Hartung melting a little around the edges. Good Lord. If she had that kind of effect on an old guy like him . . . I was afraid to turn my head and look at Aron Bodensteiner.

Aron was my boyfriend.

Well, if you can call one kiss in the boys' third-floor rest room during a basketball game with my foot caught in a toilet—if you can call that having a boyfriend, Aron was it.

He was wonderful—very tall for eighth grade, with dark hair and black-rimmed glasses. Bad skin, but I was willing to wait that out. He was very sweet and quiet and romantic, at least in my imagination. And a wonderful kisser. Of all of the *one* boys I'd ever kissed, he was the best.

I had my head turned partway around to look at him when Mr. Hartung said, "Okay, Ashley, you choose. Which of those committees would you like to be on?"

"Decorations," a voice yelled out. But it wasn't Ashley's.

It was Aron's.

Life was over.

Aron was sitting back there staring at Ashley like she was a loaded-with-everything pizza and he hadn't eaten in weeks.

He was on the decorating committee. That was why he'd said that. Here I'd been sitting on pins and needles for the last week, waiting for him to say something about taking me to the

Christmas dance. When I'd hinted in my subtle way, he'd said things like, "I'll have to go early to get the decorations up." He seemed to be assuming we'd be more or less together at the party, like a date, but it bugged me that he didn't seem all that interested in actually making a date out of it.

I had a secret suspicion that he didn't want to have to buy the corsage that is standard operating procedure around here for a dance date.

The Christmas dance was more like just a nighttime class party than an actual dance. It was supposed to be just for the eighth graders, to get us ready for society on the high school level. But usually older and younger kids leaked in, and nobody cared much.

A few couples came as couples, with corsages and all that stuff, but mostly it was just kids being delivered by their parents, in carloads. Then half the time the parents ended up hanging around all evening saying how cute we all looked, dressed up. I went last year with Neese, just to crash it and watch awhile. They had the gym all decorated and dance music going full blast, although most of the kids just sort of stood around the edges in clots, eating and drinking.

This year it was going to be different, at least that's what I'd been imagining for weeks now. I was going to have a gorgeous dress, and Aron would be my actual date, corsage and all, and it would be the start of our love. He'd look at me and realize how beautiful and unique and wonderful Dagmar Schultz was, and his heart would be mine forever.

Hah.

I dropped my head and looked at him through my hair. He'd been staring at the back of Ashley's head, but his eyes shifted to a collision course with mine. He got so red I thought his zits were going to go off like volcanoes from all that blood pressure.

He was guilty. Oh, yes. No question about that. Guilt, guilt, guilt written all over his face. He knew darn good and well that I was expecting him to be my date for that party. You don't kiss a girl in the third-floor boys' rest room unless you mean something by it.

I'd been giving him the benefit of the doubt. He was shy about going with an actual date because the other guys would tease him about me. He was broke and couldn't afford a corsage and didn't want to dishonor me by showing up empty-handed and making me go to the party empty-shouldered. Okay, that was all under-standable and forgivable.

What was *not* forgivable was his yelling out that he wanted Ashley Fingerhut on his decorating committee. And the way he was looking at her, and then turning red as a brick when I caught him at it.

I chose not to ride the bus home after school. The two curlies could just have it all to them-selves. I rode home with Neese as far as her house, since she drove to school on Mondays. It meant a two-mile walk from Neese's farm to my own house in New Berlin, but it was worth it.

The school is in Strawberry Point, in case you were confused about the travel arrangements. That's about fifteen miles from New Berlin.

It was a cold walk, with little flakes of snow drifting past in slow motion. I could catch them on my tongue if I tried. I passed the farm of my first love, James Mann. That one hadn't worked out because he hadn't switched from basketball to girls yet. But walking past his house still gave me a twinge of sadness.

And fear. Thirteen years and one month old, and already I'd lost two boyfriends.

That didn't look good. I had a whole lot of years ahead of me for getting and losing men. Until now I'd been eagerly looking forward to getting older so I could really start having love affairs.

But that was when I was sure I was going to turn out gorgeous.

Now I was just scared.

Three

I was home alone the next night when the phone rang. Well, David and Deaney were there, but that was like being alone because they never paid any attention to anyone but each other. And the baby was there, asleep in her crib with dry diapers on and a pacifier plugged into her mouth.

Mom and Daddy had gone down to Manchester to finish their Christmas shopping and taken GeorgeAnn and Cootie along. My shopping was all finished. I'd volunteered to stay home with the little kids because I didn't think it was all that much fun spending two hours dodging other family members up and down the aisles at K Mart so they wouldn't see you buying their presents.

This was the first Christmas I felt that way, and it made me wonder about myself. Maybe I was turning into a moody teenager already, only one month into my teenhood. Always before, I'd loved picking out presents for Mom and Daddy and the kids and Gramma Schultz and Neese and Aunt Gretchen, even though it was hard sticking inside the money limit and still finding something they'd want.

But this year I just couldn't seem to get into the spirit. Luckily, I'd done all my shopping a couple of weeks ago, before the gloom cloud settled on my head.

About seven-thirty Shelly called. "Hey, Daggie, you want to go down to Cedar Rapids tomorrow after school? We're going to go shopping for outfits for the Christmas dance. Me and Ashley. Mom said she'd take us. You want to come?"

What is this, I wanted to shriek in her ear. What is this want-to-come-along business? Since when does my best friend call me up at the last minute and ask if I want to tag along with her and somebody else? It was supposed to be Shelly and me planning trips to Cedar Rapids and

19

maybe asking Curlylocks, just out of politeness, if she wanted to tag along.

I gritted my back teeth and stretched the phone cord like I was getting ready to wrap it around Shelly's neck.

"Hey, Daggie. You still there?"

"I hate it when you call me Daggie, and you know it, Mickey. Mickey, Mickey, Mickey." I put all my nastiness into that one word.

"Geez, you don't have to get violent, Dag*mar*. Do you want to come along with us tomorrow or not? Or do you already have something to wear?"

"I haven't really thought about it yet," I lied airily. "It's just a class party, just the same kids we see at school every day. What's the big deal?"

"Aron Bodensteiner is the big deal," Shelly said with her killer instinct honed to the point of pain.

Casually picking at the hangnail on my thumb, I said, "So when did you and Ashley decide to go to Cedar Rapids?"

"Oh, just now. She's over here at my house, and we were looking through my closet trying to find something good to wear, and Mom just said she'd take us down to the mall after school because she wanted to look for a workout videotape for Gramma. So she said we should invite you, too, so do you want to come or not?"

Shelly's mother told her to invite me? That really hurt. I was just opening my mouth to tell her I wasn't interested in going to the mall or anyplace else with Shelly for the rest of our natural lives. But then I realized how dissatisfied I was with everything in my own closet and how exciting it would be to cruise the dress shops in the mall looking for that perfect dress to knock Aron's eyes out with.

"I'll think about it and tell you tomorrow," I said rather coolly.

I went up to my room, thinking I'd take one more look through the hangers in the stupid, impossible hope of finding something wonderful that I'd forgotten I owned. But instead, I sat down on the stool in front of the dressing table and slumped on my elbows and moped.

I wanted to cry. There was a lump in my throat, and I could almost cry, but just as I was getting warmed up to it, I started noticing something funny.

You know how sometimes you have the feeling that somebody is staring at you? You're sitting at your desk at school and you know for sure somebody behind you is staring at you. You turn around real fast, and everybody is looking down at their books, but still you know. Somebody back there was staring at you.

The feeling I had at that moment was just as eerie and just as sure. Someone else's mind was in my head, along with my own. Okay, okay, I know. Go ahead and laugh, but I could feel it there, and it was sending thoughts to me.

The bedroom door burst open, and David and Deaney came barreling in. "What were you screaming about?" David demanded.

I didn't know I'd screamed out loud, but I must have.

"Nothing," I said. They didn't need any more explanation than that.

"She just saw herself in the mirror," David explained to Deaney as they backed out of the door and pulled it shut.

"Thanks for not blowing my cover," a voice in my head whispered. "Little boys scare the bejabbers out of me."

"Who are you? *What* are you? What are you doing in my head? What am I doing talking to myself like a crazy person?"

"You're not talking to yourself—you're talking to me. I hate this part of the job, trying to convince people I exist. Just think how hard that is on the old ego, century after century, trying to

22

convince people of your existence. You think you've got problems, girl. You don't know what problems are."

I sighed and sagged and stared at the mirror with resignation. So many weird things had happened to me in the last few months that after the first shock I really didn't have any doubts at all that this thing in my head was real and was talking to me. In a Boston accent. I recognized it from hearing the Kennedys on television.

"Who and what are you?" I asked again, my voice heavy with doom. If this sort of thing was going to keep happening to me for the next sixty years, I didn't know if I could stand it.

"I am someone very famous. You've heard of me all your life. Guess."

I let out a blast of a sigh. "I'm not going to guess. Just tell me."

"No, go on, guess. I'll give you a hint. My initials are my name, and my initials are G.E.M. Does that give you a clue?"

"I'm not going to play stupid games with a voice in my head," I insisted.

"I'm the green-eyed monster," he said, pride ringing in his voice. "You know, the jealousy monster. You know, you act jealous and somebody always says, 'Green-eyed monster got you?' That's me! I'm responsible for all the jealous snits and tantrums in the world. Well, no, not the world—I just work this four-county area here in northeast Iowa, but I'm the king of snits and tantrums from Harpers Ferry to Strawberry Point. I instigate. I orchestrate."

"Get outta here," I scoffed.

"No, it's true. That's who I am, that's what I do."

I stared into my eyes in the mirror, as if I could see past them into this creature in my brain.

"Dagmar Schultz," the voice said in a self-important tone, "I have come to help you in your hour of need."

"Help me . . . how?"

"Silly girl, I'm here to help you develop your jealousy to its full potential. Help you cream that little blond sweet potato who's ruining your life."

Four

The door slammed downstairs, and my aunt Gretchen bellowed, "Anybody home?"

I bolted for the stairs. Sanity, in the form of Aunt Gretchen.

"Don't yell—the baby's asleep," I yelled.

The refrigerator door slammed. By the time I got down the stairs, Aunt Gretchen was already astride a kitchen chair, pulling at a beer.

She was my favorite relative, my mom's sister but closer to me in spirit. Mom was fat, but Gretchen was all muscle: star pitcher in the women's softball league, star bowler, book-keeper and part-time welder at the Happy Auto Body Shop.

"How's it going, Hair?" She greeted me by

jerking my hair down in back till my neck almost snapped. "Where is everybody?" she said.

"Gone down to Manchester to Christmas-shop. They'll be home pretty soon."

"Join me in a beer?"

"There wouldn't be room."

It was our same old routine. If I tried to drink a beer, Aunt Gretchen would be the first to knock me silly. The first of many relatives. I got out a bottle of Seven-Up, with a couple of inches left in the bottom, and upended it. It had been sitting without a cap for at least two days and tasted like it.

"So what are you up to?" I asked her. Aunt Gretchen lived alone in an apartment over somebody's garage. On nights when there was no bowling or softball, she often got restless and ended up at our place. My dad was one of her favorite people in the world, and so was I.

"Just bumming. What's new with you?"

That was the best thing about Aunt Gretchen: When she asked about my life, she was really asking.

"Ashley," I growled.

"Ah-ha. The cute little blond with all the hair who was out to Dean and Dorothy's Sunday for dinner, right? What's the matter—aren't you getting along?"

"Oh, we get along fine. Ashley gets along fine with everybody. She's perfect."

"Uh-huh," Aunt Gretchen said wisely. "Tell me all about it. She got your nose out of joint, has she?"

"Oh, she's just, I don't know. Horning in. She and Shelly are so buddy-buddy now, they hardly even know I'm alive. They made all these plans to go down to Cedar Rapids tomorrow after school, to shop for dresses for the class Christmas party, and they just sort of casually asked if I wanted to go along with them. Because Shelly's mom made them ask me!"

Aunt Gretchen gave me a coy grin and said, "Ah-ha, I see the green-eyed monster's got you."

"What?"

"Just a joke, Dag."

"Yeah, but why did you say that about the green-eyed monster?"

She looked at me like I was half a bubble off plumb in the sanity department.

I dropped my hands and sat back down, laughing a false, fake laugh. "Aunt Gretchen, why do people say that? Why do they say green-eyed monster when they're talking about jealousy?"

"How should I know? Who cares? People just say it, that's all. Probably because jealous people are ugly and stupid and generally unpleasant to be around. Like monsters."

Aunt Gretchen raised her beer can and held it aloft like the Statue of Liberty. That meant she was about to give me valuable advice.

"Me, I never bother to get jealous of anybody. It's a useless, destructive emotion, and it's for losers. Period. I am me, and other people are them, and I don't have to compete with anybody."

"But what about if somebody were to come along, say in your bowling league, and just wipe you out. Say some new bowler moved to town, and all of a sudden you weren't the best in the league anymore. Wouldn't you get jealous then?"

"Heck, no. I wouldn't get jealous—I'd get busy. I'd figure out how she was beating me and what I could do to improve my game. Then if I could beat her fair and square, all well and good. But if she was just flat-out better than me, then more power to her. I'd take my hat off to her. Listen, Hair, there's always going to be people around who are better bowlers than me and worse bowlers than me. There are always going to be people around who are uglier than you and prettier than you. The trick is to like yourself and respect yourself. Then it won't bother you what other people are. See?"

"Oh, sure, I see. I understand all that, but it's just . . ."

"I know. You have to live a few years and suffer through a few things like what you're going through now, before you start really genuinely understanding what I've been saying. Heck, I wasn't born this wise. I got this way by living, and there aren't any shortcuts. I can give you advice till my teeth fall out, and it won't do any good. Everybody has to learn for themselves."

"Right. But what you're saying is that I shouldn't . . . uh, listen to the green-eyed monster if he tells me to be jealous."

She looked at me curiously. "Yeah, something like that."

"Do you think there really is such a thing? A real green-eyed monster that goes around putting ideas in people's heads and making them jealous?" I was skating out onto some paper-thin ice here.

Aunt Gretchen nodded and pulled down the corners of her mouth. "Oh, sure. Right along with the Easter bunny and the tooth fairy."

"They *could* exist," I said cautiously.

"Uh-huh. And they manage to be everywhere

all at once, leaving candy eggs and swiping bloody old molars out from under pillows."

"Maybe they work territories. Like salesmen. Say, a four-county territory."

This time she looked at me with a gleam of genuine interest. "You know, Dag, you're beginning to develop a real flair for fantasy. Maybe you should be a writer when you grow up and make a million bucks with this stuff. Aliens coming out of the cornfields and taking over the bodies of all the children in town. Ta-*daa*."

She reared up out of her chair and chased me three laps around the table with her hands in strangle position. It was just lucky our baby is used to a noisy household or she'd never have slept through it.

Mom and Daddy and the rest of them came trooping in about then, dragging huge plastic K Mart bags that they tried to hide from one another.

"Okay, everybody, you know the drill," Mom said. She took all the packages away from GeorgeAnn and Cootie and Daddy and locked the packages in the downstairs bedroom closet, which had a padlock on it this time of year. Our family didn't give expensive presents, but they were at least well-kept surprises. Mom knew what everybody was giving everybody else, but none of the rest of us knew zilch, including Daddy.

They all sat around the table for a while, comparing weather notes. "Road was clear from here down to Strawberry Point, but there were some kind of glare-ice places on down south toward Manchester. No new snow, just the old stuff blowing around and glazing the road. Drifting a little bit, not too bad."

People might make fun of country people for talking about the weather so much, but when it affects everything you do, you talk about it. If the roads got too bad tonight, the trip would be off to Cedar Rapids tomorrow, to shop. And suddenly, sitting there listening to Daddy talk about glazing highways, I wanted to go tomorrow.

I didn't want to be left out anymore.

And I did want a new dress for the party.

I broke into the weather report and told Daddy about the shopping trip and asked if I could go.

"If the roads are okay. What were you planning to buy, and using what for money?"

I hung my head and looked as woebegone and appealing as possible. "I wanted something pretty to wear for the class Christmas party."

Aunt Gretchen said, "I think we've got a little competition going on here, with that new kid,

Ashley. Why don't you be a sport and give old Dag fifty bucks for some new threads?"

Daddy looked at me. "Is this important, honey? Do you absolutely have to have a new dress? It's just a class party. Don't you have something you could wear? After tonight I don't have much left in my wallet but moths. K Mart has all my worldly wealth."

I thought as hard as I could. I did have that one fancy black jersey top. "If I could just get maybe a long, pretty skirt," I said.

"Listen," Aunt Gretchen said, hauling her own billfold from the back pocket of her jeans, "you go get yourself some material, a couple of yards of something snazzy. Your mom can whip you up a long skirt in about half an hour, and I'll pop for the makings. This is your Christmas present from me, okay? Is that a deal?"

I gave her a huge hug, and to my surprise she didn't yank my hair. Instead, she sort of parted it into two long hunks and smoothed them down over my chest and kind of patted me sadly. I think she knew I was getting old.

Five

Shelly's mom picked us up at school, and we headed south toward Cedar Rapids and the mall. The glaze of ice had melted off the highway by that time, and we had smooth sailing.

At first I was a little ticked off at having to sit in front with Shelly's mom while the two curlylocks sat in back, but it was a little car, only two people wide, so it would have looked stupid if I'd tried to crowd in back with them. By rights Shelly should have had to sit in front. It was her mom. But it was too good a day to carry a grudge.

I love Cedar Rapids. It is so big and full of people. And I love shopping malls, especially at Christmas when the decorations are so gorgeous and everybody is in such a good mood. But most of all, I love buying stuff!

There was never any extra money at our house. My dad works a lot of different jobs, like driving the town snowplow in winter and the town weed mower in summer, and helping out at the gas station when they get busy, and driving a stock truck for the livestock sale barn when they need him. And then he hunts a lot, out at Uncle Dean's farm, and runs a trap line. But still he never has any extra money, and I know better than to ask if it's not for an important cause.

Daddy told me once that he and Mom decided a long time ago that they'd rather have lots of kids than be rich. He said we kids were the treasure in our family. I find that pretty hard to believe about GeorgeAnn and Cootie, but I'm sure Mom and Daddy think it's true.

The point is, shopping binges at the mall are a fantasy of mine. I've been trying to build up a baby-sitting business, but so far nothing much has happened. Everybody we know around New Berlin has relatives they leave their kids with, for free. So my dreams about running wild through Sears and Younkers, gathering skirts and shoes and belts and blouses left and right—well, they're still dreams.

There's something so exciting and satisfying about adding a thing to your life. A red leather belt, say. It's more than just the belt; owning it is some kind of step up in the world. If I tried to explain this to Mom or Daddy, they'd give me heck for being selfish and materialistic and not knowing what was important in life.

They'd probably be right. All I know is, every time I can add some new little bit to what belongs to me, it's like I've gotten a little more, I don't know, important, maybe. More like a real person. An adult, running her own life and doing what she wants.

That's a lot to get from a red leather belt.

It was almost dark when we finally found a parking place at the mall. It was a huge mall with miles of parking, but every slot was full, up and down every row. Santas were ringing bells at the entrance doors, and "I Heard the Bells on Christmas Day" was playing over the sound system.

I was getting so much in the mood, I forgot to be jealous and jostled happily up against Shelly and Ashley in the crowd. We took a quick vote and decided to eat first, shop later. At the main intersection of mall branches, there were a bunch of small tables around a fountain where Santa was on duty. All around the tables were booths selling everything you could think of to eat, from Orange Julius to Taco John to Tater Skins to pizza boats.

I used some of my precious skirt money for a big fat taco bravo. Ashley followed me, asked what a taco bravo was, and ordered one, too. I was ridiculously flattered.

Maybe she's not so bad after all, I thought, in my new warm and happy mood.

But when we got back to the tables, which were only big enough for two people, Shelly waved Ashley over to her table, and I was stuck sitting with her mom. I tried to keep up with what Shelly and Ashley were talking about at their table, but most of it was so low I couldn't hear it. And then they'd start laughing and kind of cutting their eyes sideways toward me.

Shelly's mom kept trying to talk to me. "Remember to check on the width of the material, Dagmar. If you get a fifty-four-inch-wide fabric, you won't need more than a yard, even for a floor-length skirt. And have the clerk get what you need for the belt. Or do you want me to come with you? Dagmar?"

But I wasn't listening. All I could hear was the two of them whispering and laughing over at that other table . . . and the small insistent voice of

G.E.M. "Get even with her," he whispered. "Get her."

We separated after we ate. I headed downstream in the flood of people, toward the So Fro Fabric Shop, and the rest of them went the other way. It didn't take long to find what I wanted. It was love at first sight, and it was half-price on the remnant table, a yard and a half of blue-green velveteen the color of a peacock's tail. I held it up and imagined it as a floor-length skirt swirling dramatically around my ankles, with my black jersey top.

It was a bolt-end remnant with a flawed place at one corner, so it was lots cheaper than I'd figured, even with the thread and zipper and matching belt kit. I had enough left over for a string of matching colored beads from the boutique next door. The beads were turquoise-colored chunks of wood on a gold chain, and they looked lots more expensive than $3.98.

I headed upstream again, toward the stores most likely to attract Shelly and Ashley, people who could just go out and buy a new dress, money no object, instead of having to make do with an old jersey top and a homemade skirt.

I stopped and shook my head. Where had that

thought come from? Just a minute ago I'd been thrilled spitless with my skirt material and necklace, and here I was, all of a sudden, resenting Shelly and Ashley for having the money for new dresses.

Just then I saw Ashley and Shelly over by the bakery counter, talking to the cutest boy I'd ever seen in my entire life. He was tall and tan, with blond curly hair and a smile that would melt your bones.

He was looking down at Ashley, just looking down at her and grinning as if he couldn't get enough of her. And she was sort of twinkling up at him and chatting away a mile a minute.

I got over there just as he was leaving.

"Who was that?" I managed to get the words out casually.

"Oh, just this boy from my old school. Eric."

Shelly's voice had a definite squeak in it. "Was he your boyfriend? Did you go out with him?"

"Oh, once or twice. I didn't really like him all that well. He's kind of conceited."

Of course he's conceited, I thought. He's perfect. Why wouldn't he be aware of the fact?

I tagged silently after them through three small dress shops and a department store, sitting on little velvet chairs and thinking dark thoughts while Shelly and Ashley disappeared into dressing room after dressing room.

The dark thoughts that filled my head were mine, all mine this time. It was not fair. It was just plain flat-out not fair for one person to have as much as Ashley had—the new-girl advantage, hair better than mine, an undeniable waistline, Shelly drooling all over her, *my boyfriend* drooling all over her, and now Eric. The guy was an absolute god, and she had discarded him as not good enough for her. She had *discarded* a boy I could never even have aspired to.

I hated her.

"Dag? What do you think?"

I looked up. Ashley was standing in the open doorway to the dressing rooms, looking expectant.

She was wearing a coral pink velvet dress, short and straight as a tube but cut off straight across, just above her boobs. All that held it up were two narrow spaghetti straps tied with bows on her shoulders.

I felt the stirring in the back of my mind, but I was way ahead of old G.E.M. this time.

I knew what I was going to do, and it was beautiful!

"It's perfect," I called to her. "Buy it."

Shelly agreed, and in short order the pink dress was tissue tucked, boxed in a holiday box, and charged on her daddy's charge card.

The charge card business would have made me jealous all by itself . . . but now I didn't need to be jealous of her. I had a master plan, and it was beautiful.

Ashley Fingerhut would never be able to show her face in my school again.

Six

The next morning before school I pinned Aron to the wall, or rather to the locker.

"Are you taking me to the party or not?" I said. "You're supposed to be my boyfriend. I've been sitting around all week expecting you to say something about it, and you haven't, so don't blame me for coming right out and asking. You forced me into it."

He looked so scared and uncomfortable I almost took pity on him. But not quite.

"Gee, Dag, I guess I figured . . . see, I have to be there early to put up the last-minute decorations. I have to pick up some garlands and other stuff from the greenhouse and take them over to the gym. So I can't take a date, see."

41

I looked at him askance. I'm not sure what askance means, but it sounds like the way I felt. Like I didn't buy his story.

"They won't wait till the last minute to put up garlands, Aron."

"Well, no, maybe not the actual garlands, but some of that other stuff that would wilt if they put it up too soon."

"Crepe paper?"

"No. Of course not. Poinsettias and stuff like that."

I thought about it. "The last poinsettia we got for Christmas was still going strong in July, Aron."

"I got to get going. The bell's about to ring."

"So in other words, you're not taking a date. Any date. Right?"

"Right."

"Not me, not Ashley Fingerhut, not anybody, right?"

"Well, yes and no."

"What's that supposed to mean, Aron?"

"Well, Ashley's on the committee, so I'll probably give her a ride over as a committee member." He nodded and smiled, like he'd just talked himself out of the firing squad.

The bell rang, so I had to let it go at that.

Obviously I was going to be on my own, party night.

But that was okay.

I grinned an evil grin and ran for my classroom just as the door was being pulled shut.

* * *

As of Saturday morning, the big day, Mom still hadn't started making my skirt. I was getting a little nervous about it and mentioned it to her seventy-eleven times. But when she finally did open up the old Singer, she had that skirt whipped up in about half an hour. She left the hem for me to do, but that was okay. It helped make the afternoon go faster.

Neese drove over around suppertime, to put on my finishing touches and to drive me to the party. She'd offered, saying it might be fun to hang around awhile and watch the younger generation. What that translated into was that she was hoping a few of the older guys her age would show up.

She brought her whole collection of eye makeup and blusher, and three professional curling irons from her mother's beauty shop. One thing I will say about my cousin Neese is that she can do the best eye makeup of anybody I know. My eyelids matched the turquoise of the skirt, but with silvery glittery stuff that even stuck to the mascara. We were going to see if we could get away with false eyelashes, but Mom checked up on us partway through the process.

"No false eyelashes. No mascara. And get that sparkly stuff off her, Neese. You should have better sense than that. The child is thirteen, not thirty."

"How about a fake mole, then, for a beauty spot by the corner of her mouth?" Neese said, always the optimist.

Mom heaved a huge sigh and closed the door on us. We took that to mean okay for the beauty spot. It felt funny, stuck on my face like unlicked food, but Neese swore it made me look sexy, so I left it on.

We got to the school gym just as they were turning down the lights and turning up the music. All decorations were in place, all garlands garlanding out from the light fixtures. Nothing looked as though it had been done at the last minute.

It was beautiful. Winter Wonderland was the theme, and it really did look more like a winter wonderland than a junior high gym where I spent three hours a week chasing a volleyball and getting elbows in the eye. There were life-

44

size cardboard pine trees with cotton snow around them, and jillions of cut-out snowflakes hanging from strings all over the place, and even a cardboard full moon over the refreshment table.

I was relieved to see some other long skirts here and there. I'd been afraid of having the only one. I looked all around the room, trying to spot Ashley, Aron, Shelly. But the shadows of the snowflakes made it hard to see anything very well.

Neese grabbed me and started dancing. I hated dancing with my girl cousin, it made it so obvious that I didn't have anybody better to dance with. But I knew how petrified she got, walking into a room full of people. She had to do something instantly, even if it was something stupid.

It was a fast dance, though, so we could pretend we weren't dancing with each other. Neese and I had been practicing our dance moves for two years now, so we were both pretty good in motion.

We stayed on the dance floor a long time, me searching for my friends and enemies, Neese searching for sophomore or even freshman boys. She wouldn't turn up her nose at a freshman if he showed any interest in her.

Shelly danced past, with Matthew, who was her more-or-less boyfriend. They didn't have dates or anything—they just rode around town on his four-wheeler a lot, and that made them sort of a couple. His dad had driven them tonight and was now standing out in the hall with some other fathers, talking crops or deer hunting or whatever.

It wasn't till almost nine that I spotted Ashley. It was a slow dance, where you have to have an actual partner, so Neese had disappeared toward the rest rooms. I was dancing with Dickie Arney, who hadn't had his growth spurt yet, so he was about a full head shorter than me. He also didn't know beans about leading. I had to do all the steering and, besides that, I didn't like the fact that he was eye level with my bra. But it was better than pretending to have to go to the rest room every time a slow dance came along.

At least Dickie gave me an unblocked view of the room. And there she was, pink velvet dress, cascade of curly yellow hair, and my boyfriend bending down to dance close.

It almost made me sick, watching them. What good was the turquoise long velvet skirt and the chunky beads and the eye makeup anyway? Aron hadn't gotten close enough to see me all night, and if he had, he wouldn't have noticed me. All he could see was that darn Ashley.

Okay, I told myself, this is it.

No, I argued. It's a dirty trick. It's beneath my dignity. I shouldn't do it.

But that little voice at the back of my mind said, "Get her, Dagmar. She's got it coming."

Luckily, Dickie was easy to steer. With a few flashy turns I had him over close to Aron and Ashley.

Aron and Ashley. Even their names sounded as if they went together. It was sickening.

I hunched my shoulders and shook my head a little. Dickie never took his eyes off my chest.

There she was, in all her pink and gold glory, with her back to me. Just an easy reach away.

Okay, okay, I told myself. I'm really going to do it now.

Okay. Now. Quick before the music ends.

I got my hand loose from Dickie's and gave a casual rub to my nose. Then, quick and smooth as a snake striking, my hand darted out, brushed through Ashley's hair, and found its target.

One pull on the spaghetti strap bow, and it was loose. A second snake strike on the other shoulder, a quick, hard pull, and it was over.

Ashley froze. The pink dress slid to the floor.

Aron went on dancing a couple more steps, too astounded to stop his feet.

There stood Ashley Fingerhut in front of God and the whole eighth grade, in nothing but a head of hair and white pantyhose.

Dickie and I jammed to a halt along with all the rest of the freeway pileup. It seemed like a lifetime that we all stood staring at her, but it was really only about a second and a half.

She was supposed to run screaming off the floor and die of embarrassment in the rest room, and then go home and beg her father to move back to Cedar Rapids.

Only she didn't.

She did a fast squat, pulled the dress back up into place, and, with a toss of her hair, retied the shoulder straps.

"Oops," she said with an easy, sunny laugh. And that was it. *That was it.*

She and Aron started dancing again; the crowd started laughing and talking and even clapping for her. She just grinned and waved them away and concentrated her attention on Aron.

Aron Bodensteiner, the one boy I'd thought I could count on. The one I chose for my boyfriend out of the whole school, not two months ago.

He was dancing like he was in a coma, his feet

barely shuffling. He looked as if he'd been pole-axed by what he'd just seen.

He looked like a man in love permanently and hopelessly.

Way to go, Dagmar, I thought in disgust. Dismay and disgust. Hopeless dismay, disgust, and distemper. No, that was for dogs.

I became aware that Dickie was saying something into my chest.

"Wow," he breathed. "Wow. Wow. Wow."

Well, if Ashley hadn't been the belle of the ball before, I had certainly helped her along. From now on she could sell raffle tickets just for a chance to walk her to class.

The only incredibly narrow silver lining to my dark cloud was that nobody seemed to suspect me of doing the untying. From what I gathered, eavesdropping on the conversations around me, the dropping of the dress was a pure act of God. A blessing from the patron saint of teenage boys.

Seven

Sunday morning. I buried my head in my pillow and tried to die. It would be so much easier than getting up, going to church, listening to everybody talking about what had happened at the junior high dance when that sweet little new girl's dress fell off right in the middle of the dance floor and she just took it all in stride like a little trouper.

Mom yelled up at me to get up and get dressed. I yelled back that I wanted to stay in bed. Daddy came up and sat on the bed and felt my forehead.

"I'm not sick," I growled. "I just don't feel like getting out of bed this morning." I wanted to pull away from his loving kindness and bury myself in the pillow again . . . and I wanted to throw myself in his arms and bawl like a baby, for no reason I could name.

Daddy grinned at me and popped out his false teeth. He had false teeth in front, and he could slip them out on his tongue and pop them back in again. He used to do it all the time for me when I was little, to make me laugh when I was bawling over a scraped knee.

"That doesn't work anymore, Daddy." I was surprised at the sadness in my voice, and so was he. For an instant he looked about like I felt.

Then he made himself cheer up, and said, "You want to tell me what's got you lower than a hole in the ground this morning?"

"No. But thanks for asking. It isn't anything. It's just life."

"Oh. Yeah. That one. Well, life can look pretty dismal from time to time. It always gets better."

"But then it always gets worse again."

He grinned. "Yeah, but then it gets better again."

"Don't try to cheer me up, Daddy. I just want to be alone awhile. I'm not ready to start joking around yet."

He thought about that for a minute, then stood up and patted my foot under the blanket.

"Okay, kid. No law says you have to get up

and go to church. But we'll expect you to be ready to go out to Dean and Dorothy's for dinner as usual, after church. Too much moping around isn't good for you. It gets to be a habit."

GeorgeAnn appeared in the bedroom door. "You have to go to church this morning, Dagmar. You'll miss 'Angels We Have Heard on High.'"

GeorgeAnn had been driving everybody nuts for two weeks now, practicing the big number she was singing as a solo in Angel Choir this morning. It had some Latin words in it, and she loved singing foreign words even when she had no idea what they meant.

Mom came up the stairs after breakfast to look in on me and feel my forehead. By the time they finally left for church, I was beginning to think it would have been easier to get up and get dressed and go along with them, instead of explaining over and over that I wasn't sick, I just didn't feel like getting up.

And facing the day, and the rest of my life. I didn't say that to anybody, but it was what I felt. It seemed as if I was wrapped in heavy blankets that covered my face and pinned down my arms, and I couldn't fight free from them. And all the rest of my life was going to be the same.

I dragged myself over to my dressing table to

see if I looked awful in the mirror. My hair was a giant rat's nest, and my eye makeup was half worn off and half smudged. I'd been in too bad a mood last night to wash my face when I went to bed, and now I was paying the price.

I sighed. I couldn't believe I'd done such a stupid thing, as untying Ashley's straps out there in front of everybody. I just felt . . . cruddy.

"Miserable, weepy, depressed?" said a familiar voice in my head. "Suicide. There's your answer."

"Get out of here!" I picked up the Kleenex box and threw it at my own face in the mirror.

"As Daddy said, things always get better. I don't even know why I'm feeling this down, if you want to know the truth. Sure, last night was a disaster, but nobody knows I had anything to do with it, so I'm not in trouble over it. It's just so . . ."

"Depressing," replied the voice. "You're depressed because somebody came along who is prettier than you are, nicer than you are, more popular than you, and all the boys are nuts over her. She's stolen your best friend and your boyfriend. Of course, I didn't mean that you should actually *do* it, just threaten to do it. Start to do it. Act as if you're going to do it, and just watch. You'll be flooded with more loving attention than you ever dreamed of. Take my word. It can't fail. It never does."

Flooded with loving attention?

That sounded wonderful. I began thinking . . . what if I got hurt? What if I had some almost-terrible near-accident that didn't really cause pain and suffering but generated a ton of sympathy? Wouldn't it be dramatic and romantic to be lying in a hospital bed all weak and pale, Aron Bodensteiner coming to see me with flowers? He'd kneel beside my bed and whisper, "Dagmar, I didn't know I cared so deeply about you. It's you I really love. Ashley was just a passing flirtation. She's much too shallow for me. Please get well again, and we'll go to every dance together for the rest of our lives." And then he'd kiss me and forget all about Ashley.

I got back in bed and lay there for the rest of the morning, just thinking, planning, discarding plans, and taking them up again.

If I could arrange it so I wouldn't actually hurt myself, something like a broken leg might be the answer after all. As an attention-getter you couldn't beat a huge cast.

The trick would be to make sure I didn't get badly hurt, or kill myself, trying for the broken leg.

I started wondering how much a broken bone

really did hurt, and for how long. Maybe a sprained ankle would do the trick.

Then I started wondering if, instead of having to suffer any actual pain at all, I could just have a near miss. No, that probably wouldn't be enough to get me any real lasting supply of love and sympathy.

What if word got out that I was going to jump off the bridge? Of course, in the dead of winter, the river would be frozen, but what better way to break a leg?

By the time the family got back from church, I had just about decided to give it a try. And I knew just how to go about it.

Eight

After the usual huge Sunday dinner, most of us went outside. Gramma Schultz had her nap, Mom and Aunt Dorothy did dishes, but the rest of us went out into the dazzling, snowy sunshine. The whole farm, the whole world, was silvery white with blue shadows.

It seemed like a dumb time to be talking about jumping off bridges, but if I was going to go through with it, it would have to be fast, before I lost my nerve. And the first step in the plan was getting Neese alone.

Daddy and Uncle Dean and Cootie uncovered the snowmobile in the side yard and fiddled around with it till they got it running. They ran it about three times each winter, and it always

56

took more fiddling than it was worth, in my opinion. Take out spark plugs and wipe them off and test them, that kind of stuff. But men love it.

Once they got it going, Uncle Dean took each of us for a ride, along the ditch between the road and the fences, into the pasture, uphill and downhill, along the frozen creek bed and bouncing up over its bank.

I went first, then Neese. Then they got all three of the guys on at the same time, Uncle Dean and Daddy with Cootie sandwiched in between them, and away they roared, down the hayfield lane, into the timber road, and out of sight.

Neese and I sat side by side on the stone retaining wall along the edge of the yard. Their house was a big old square thing made of yellowish blocks of limestone, like the wall we sat on. The dairy barn was stone, too, and a couple of the smaller buildings. Rows of tall pines sheltered the house on the north and west sides and made a nice dark green frame for it. It was lots better than our house in town, even though Aunt Dorothy had a beauty shop in the downstairs bedroom.

The wall made a good place to sit. It was warmed by the sun, and we could see anybody who happened to drive by. Neese spent lots of time watching for somebody interesting to drive by. I had the feeling she was going to be doing that all her life.

Depressing. My dark mood rolled over me again, for no reason I could pinpoint. Neese wasn't pretty, and she was sixteen and had never had a single boyfriend. I'd always assumed I was better than Neese, but now . . .

Maybe Neese and I would grow old together, just sitting on this stone wall and hoping in vain for that interesting person to drive by.

I heard myself saying the words I'd been rehearsing all through dinner. "If I tell you something, will you swear you won't tell a soul?"

"Of course," Neese lied eagerly.

"I've decided to jump off the bridge."

"Get out of here," she scoffed, whamming me with her elbow.

"No, I mean it. Tonight at nine o'clock I'm going to jump off the New Berlin Bridge."

"But why? Dagmar, where did you get such a stupid idea? That river's frozen solid. You could break a leg. You know, sometimes you make me sick. You gripe and bitch about your little problems, and you don't know how lucky you are. You're not fat, you know how to talk to boys, you've already had three boyfriends, and you're barely thirteen. Why would you . . ."

Something in her voice caught my attention. I was so wrapped up in my own blues I almost missed the message, but suddenly I understood what she was thinking. Even though I hadn't said a word about suicide, or even thought it, the idea of it hung in the air between us like the white clouds of our breath.

Neese herself had considered suicide. I knew it. I could hear it in what she wasn't saying. My throat lumped up, and I gave her a hug, but she didn't know how to read it.

"Why would you want to jump off the bridge, Dagmar?" She stared at me, scared out of her wits.

By now I was wishing I hadn't started this whole thing. "I have problems nobody knows about," I said. "Depressions."

"You? Dagmar Schultz, depressed? I don't believe it."

"Believe it."

"Dagmar, please don't do it. Please don't."

I wanted to comfort her and tell her I had no real intention of hurting myself, that I just needed a whole lot more love than I was getting at the moment. But I couldn't say that.

We just sat side by side on that stone wall with our arms around each other, staring off down the road, till the snowmobile roared back into the yard and the moment was shattered by its noise.

* * *

It was late afternoon by the time we'd delivered Gramma Schultz back to the Lutheran Home and driven home again through a snowy twilight.

I spent the whole trip hunched in my corner of the backseat, not saying a word to anybody. Telling Neese I was going to jump off the bridge was one of my more colossal dumb tricks. I knew that by the time we sat down to supper.

But my funny mood was still there, too, that feeling of wanting to cry for no good reason, wanting somebody to hug me and make a fuss over me and stroke my hair. I said I wasn't hungry, which was true, and got up from the table.

Mom caught up with me in my room. She's so heavy that it's hard for her to climb the stairs, and she doesn't come up unless she has to. GeorgeAnn and I do all the upstairs housecleaning, and usually it's Daddy who checks on the boys to be sure they're sleeping and not playing.

She was puffing for breath as she leaned over my bed, lifted my hair, and peered at my face.

"What's the matter with you today? Are you sick?"

"No," I whined.

"Then what?"

"I don't know. I just feel like, I don't know. Crummy."

Tears started coming in my eyes, and that scared me. There really was something wrong with me. I wasn't just putting it on. There really was some dark depression inside me, making me cry for no reason.

I think if Mom had sat down on the bed right then and held me and let me cry, that would have been all I needed. But she didn't. She straightened up and started toward the door. I could hear Delight fussing in her high chair down in the kitchen. Delight, the baby. Naturally she would come first in Mom's book.

"Well, if you're not sick, then quit feeling sorry for yourself and straighten up, Dagmar. There's no call for all this silliness."

I lay there on the bed for a long time, churning and boiling away inside. It was like a regular battle down in the bottom of my stomach, and it made me ache with actual pain.

I felt cut off from the rest of the family. They were down there having an ordinary Sunday

61

night, just like everything was normal. The phone rang a few times, the television was on loud, the little kids were on louder, and GeorgeAnn was clanging away on the piano.

It was like they didn't even miss me.

What good was a black, depressed mood if nobody even cared?

Nine o'clock on the bridge; that was what I'd told Neese. I was going to jump off the bridge at nine o'clock. It was almost eight-thirty.

I dragged myself up off the bed and pulled on my warmest sweat suit. Not that I was really going to jump off a bridge, of course, but still I might have to stand on it for a while. Might as well be warm.

As I came downstairs, Mom and Daddy turned to look at me. I pulled on my boots and parka by the front door.

"Going out?" Daddy said.

"Just going for a walk."

They looked at each other but didn't try to stop me. I thought they might. I thought one of those phone calls might have been from Neese, warning them, and if so, they wouldn't let me leave.

But they did.

I walked down the front steps, down the sidewalk, then down the middle of the street that ended half a block later at the bridge.

Nobody stopped me. That meant Neese didn't care enough about me to call and warn them, or they didn't care enough to be worried. If I'd been in a logical mood, I would have known that wasn't true, but right then I didn't feel logical. I felt rotten.

The reasons weren't even very clear anymore. Was it just Ashley? Just my jealousy toward her? Or the rotten, sick way I felt when the jealousy rolled over me and made me do and say stupid stuff?

Or was it that deep-down fear that life was just going to be one Ashley after another, always somebody prettier and nicer than I was, to take away my friends and lovers? All that pain waiting for me . . .

The bridge was empty. It was blocked off on both ends by a wooden fence to keep cars off. Some bridge authority had found cracks in it awhile back, and neither the town nor the county wanted to claim ownership of the bridge and have to pay for fixing it. So they just closed it. Somebody had stuck a basketball hoop up on one end, so it had been a basketball court all fall. Before that it was a good place to sit and dangle your legs over and watch kids wading in the river below. Some people tried to fish off it but never caught anything much.

The Volga River was about twenty feet wide at that point, and maybe two or three feet deep, with a nice, clean, sand bottom. Shelly and I had spent many a summer day sitting in the water and sending bits of twigs and leaves floating away downstream.

That thought only made me sadder, as I leaned on the bridge rail and looked down.

It was a long way down there, and the ice looked very, very hard.

Nine

I was about to turn and trudge back up the hill toward home when I heard footsteps squeaking in the snow. Daddy, with Mom puffing along behind him, was coming down the hill fast.

A car's headlights showed up, on the quarry road, coming from the direction of Uncle Dean's.

I turned and looked the other way, toward Main Street on the far side of the bridge. Shelly was running toward me, and Ashley behind her. And Charlie, the old guy who gives me such a hard time every chance he gets. And a bunch of other people from around town.

Neese had called people! She did care enough about me to call and spread the word, not only to Mom and Daddy but apparently to half the town, too. And everybody was coming to tell me they loved me.

Or else to stand around in a circle pointing at me and laughing their heads off at my stupidity.

I felt like a trapped rabbit there in the middle of the bridge with Uncle Dean's headlights glaring at me through the barrier.

Shelly was the fastest runner. She got to me first and threw her arms around me. "Don't do it, don't jump," she sobbed.

"Boy, word gets around fast, doesn't it?" I said. "What did Neese do, call the whole town?"

"Just about," Shelly said, snuffling. She held me off and stared at me, with something like compassion on her face. The black mood began to lift just a shade.

Daddy was there by that time, grabbing my elbow. "Dagmar, what is this nonsense about wanting to hurt yourself? That's the silliest thing you've ever done. After all the loving and caring you've gotten from this family! Do you know how lucky you are? Do you have any idea how many kids your age would kill to get into a family like ours? Do you?"

I stared at him, my mouth hanging open. He was really mad. He was furious, in fact. It was the first time in my whole life I'd ever seen him truly mad at anybody, for anything.

And here I'd always thought Daddy and I had something special going between us. Even though he was careful not to have an obvious favorite, I still thought I was the one he liked being with the most.

My black cloud just swamped me. I stood there staring at him, barely noticing a scraping sound from under the bridge.

"I'm going to jump," I said, to hurt him. For the first time I actually saw myself doing it, standing on the bridge railing and jumping off. "You don't love me," I wailed.

Mom and Daddy both crowded toward me, getting into each other's way. "Of course we love you, fathead," Daddy yelled at me.

Old Charlie back in the crowd said, "These kids nowadays expect everything handed to them. Expect to be loved even though there ain't a blessed blue-eyed thing about them that's lovable. I remember back when I was a boy—"

"Shut up, Charlie," someone said.

"You can have Aron back," Ashley called from behind Shelly. "I didn't want him all that much anyhow. You can have him back."

That really frosted me.

Neese crowded forward and reached toward me like she was going to say something, but she didn't. She just looked me in the eyes long and

67

deep and sad, and once again I knew that she was the one with enough genuine unhappiness to be doing what I was doing.

Doing? Was I really going to jump? My heart started pounding.

I took a step toward the railing, straddled it, but couldn't make myself look down. Out of the corner of my eye, I thought I saw a flash of movement down there, and again I heard the scraping sound.

Daddy said, "Dagmar Schultz, you get over here right now. Get away from that railing. You're causing a whole lot of trouble and worry for folks who don't deserve it. And you're being silly besides. There is nothing wrong with your life—you're just too young to know how lucky you are. I never knew you to be this selfish before."

That did it. If I couldn't count on Daddy . . . I just wanted to punish the whole world at that instant.

I threw my other leg over the railing, closed my eyes, and jumped.

* * *

A whoosh of cold air . . . a landing like jumping on a mattress from standing on the footboard of the bed. Cold and wet, but soft. I went in feet first, hit with hardly even a jar up my leg bones, and came to rest waist-deep in a snowbank.

I opened my eyes and saw Uncle Dean and Aunt Dorothy standing on the ice, leaning against snow-shovel handles and puffing for breath. Behind them were three other people from town, also with shovels.

"Well," Uncle Dean said with a suggestion of a twinkle in his voice, "did that take care of the problem, Daggie?"

The funny thing was, it had. I stood there belly deep in snow so I couldn't move, with all my family and friends looking down at me from the bridge, and suddenly I started laughing. I couldn't help myself.

Shelly and Ashley started giggling, Charlie gave a croaky hoot, and pretty soon everybody on the bridge was laughing at me. But not at me, more like with me. I could feel a big round glow of warmth and love around me. It was weird, and I can't really describe it, but it was like there was a shift in the universe, and everything that had seemed out of kilter for me lately just fell back into place.

Mom was crying. I could hear her crying and laughing at the same time. Cootie appeared from somewhere and was standing on the edge of the bridge, leaning way out above me.

"I want to jump, too," he was chanting over and over.

"You're not going to jump," Daddy said, but Uncle Dean called up to him. "It's okay, we got a nice big bank of snow piled up here. He can't hurt himself, no more than jumping in a pile of leaves in the fall."

So Cootie copied my leap, and then Matthew Garms and then Shelly. I had to get out of the way so they didn't land on me. Uncle Dean and Aunt Dorothy hauled me out and hugged me, then turned to haul out the next jumper.

I started up the hill toward home but turned for a last look. Daddy was hanging out over the edge of the bridge, getting ready to take his turn. I just shook my head and plowed on home.

Ten

When I woke up the next morning, the answer to my strange mood was there before my eyes. A spot of blood on the sheet.

I was a woman!

Finally, at last, hooray, whoopee, I was a woman!

I'd been waiting for this moment for two years, ever since Shelly got her first period and Mom sat me down with the pamphlet telling about "those special days."

I'd tried to pump Shelly for information, but she didn't like talking about it. It embarrassed her. Same with Neese. Mom would have answered my questions if I'd asked her directly, and I did once or twice. I'd asked her what

71

cramps were like, and she'd said she didn't know—she never had them. I'd asked her if she hated having periods, and she'd just sort of smiled softly and hugged me and said, no, periods were a tiny price to pay for having six beautiful babies.

And now I'd joined the club.

It was early morning of the first day of Christmas vacation. GeorgeAnn was still sound asleep on her side of the room, and nobody else was awake yet either, not even the baby.

I knew I'd have to get up in a minute and take care of things, tell Mom the wonderful news, get her to take me to the store for supplies of my own.

But just for a minute I lay back against the pillow and smiled. I wanted G.E.M. to tune in so I could tell him that stupid old jealousy had been nothing more than premenstrual moodiness.

He didn't, and suddenly somehow I knew he wouldn't, ever again. He probably never had, I realized.

Young children have such vivid imaginations. . . .